THE GARDEN FROG AND THE MONGREL DOG

WRITTEN BY LARISSA CHARLES
ILLUSTRATED BY ANN CHARLES

THE GARDEN FROG AND THE MONGREL DOG

Written by Larissa Charles

Illustrated by Ann Charles

Book Design by Joleene Naylor

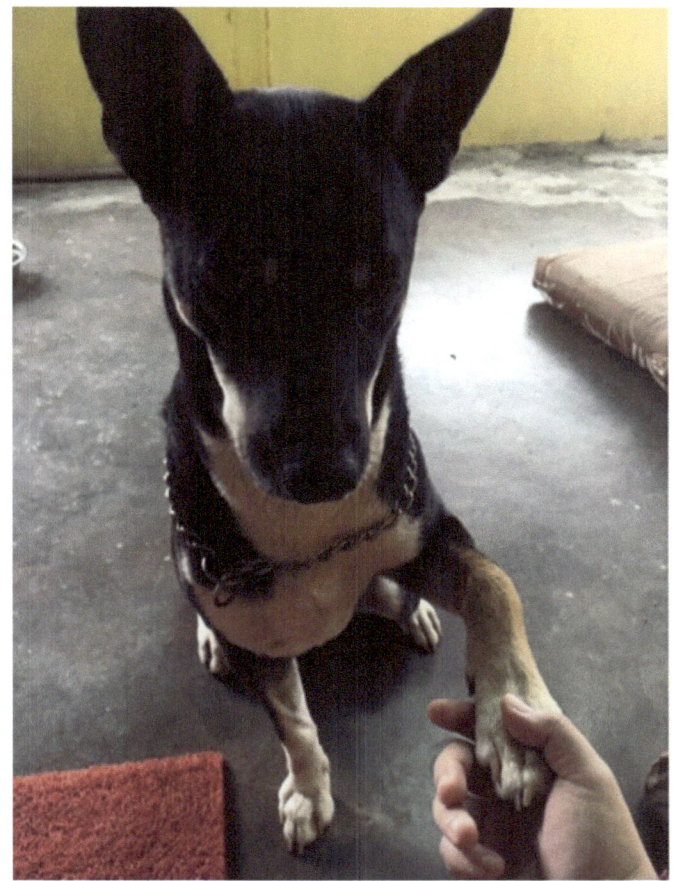

This book is dedicated to my mongrel dog, Jango and all the beautiful wildlife of Malaysia.

One evening, the clouds hung low and gray.
Thunder and lightning shook up every creature in their place of stay.

Fast asleep in his underground lair, was a speckled frog who lived without a care.
But the commotion in the air, made the garden frog aware that
it was a thunderstorm scare!

Looking around and searching for safe ground,
it made its way to the veranda floor straight away.

Lying horizontal on the floor, was a bamboo pole.
The garden frog leapt towards it. Not knowing what was yet to come!!!

As it sat upon the pole, it was soon covered in drool.

Ruff! Ruff! Barked the mongrel.
Baring its teeth and staring beneath, not giving a chance for the frog to leap.

The frog shut its eyes in fright while the dog barked at it with delight.

The dog nuzzled against the frog
as the frog huddled against the rim of the bamboo log.
The dog scratched the floor with its claw, skreeekk! skreeekk! The frog froze!

The little frog did not move at all. The dog began to cautiously lick it.
Smick! Smick!
To the frog's appall........

...the dog curled its tongue with dislike of the taste. Ick! Ick!

Once again, the dog put its wet nose on the frog and took a whiff. Sniff! Sniff!
Then, it barked at the damp creature curiously. Arrf! Arrf!

The frog was tired of the dog's mischief, so it tried to leave.
But the dog chased the frog and gave it grief!

The frog leapt to the left, the dog scuttled there and stared.

The frog leapt to the right, the dog shuttled there and sneered!

The growling and prowling of the dog went on and on.

The poor little frog hopped to and fro on the veranda floor...

....to find a way out into the lawn.

Suddenly, lightning flashed, and thunder crashed.
The dog was startled and made a dash.
It scampered to the entrance of the house. Scrimple! Scrample!

A tree branch struck by lightning snapped.

Kaboom! Kabang! The dog was stuck under it completely bashed!

It whimpered in pain under the rain. Nnnn! Nnnn!

This was to the frog's gain as it happily leapt back into the lawn
and into a humungous monsoon drain.

The battered dog did not give up. After the rain, he searched for the frog again.
To his misfortune, it was nowhere to be found!
He stood baffled by the fence as he tried to make sense. Oh, what a suspense!